THE
DANCE
OF THE
DINOSAURS

First published in paperback in Great Britain by Collins Picture Books in 2002

1 3 5 7 9 10 8 6 4 2   ISBN: 0-00-711444-3

Collins Picture Books is an imprint of the Children's Division,

part of HarperCollins Publishers Ltd.

Text and illustrations copyright © Colin & Jacqui Hawkins 2002

The author/illustrators assert the moral right to
be identified as the author/illustrators of the work.

A CIP catalogue record for this title is available from the British Library.

The HarperCollins website address is
www.**fire**and**water**.com

Printed and bound in China.

THE
DANCE
OF THE
DINOSAURS

Colin and Jacqui Hawkins

Collins

An Imprint of HarperCollins Publishers

Lightning flashed on a wild, stormy night
And Georgie and Dee shivered in fright.

"Come on," said Cat. "Don't be afraid!
I'll show you both how a storm is made."

As the thunder roared and rumbled
Down the stairs after Cat they tumbled.

"Where are we going?" cried Georgie to Dee.
"Hurry," called Cat. "Wait and see!"

They chased down the garden after Cat.
The wind lashed the trees this way and that.

"Look!" yelled Dee. "There's a balloon!"
"Be quick!" called Cat, "it's going soon."

They jumped aboard – just in time –
As higher and higher they started to climb.

Cat sailed the balloon through the dark night,
Then a strange land came into sight.

Down they flew through the raging sky,
Great flying lizards went swooping by.

"Look!" cried Dee, "at those beaks and claws."
And Georgie yelled, "They're DINOSAURS!"

As the balloon landed on the ground,
Enormous Dinosaurs lumbered around.

"Oh!" said Georgie, "I don't like it here!"
"Come on," said Cat, "there's nothing to fear."

"Follow me," grinned Cat, "don't be afraid,
Now, this is how a storm is made."

The Dance of the Dinosaurs had begun
So they all joined in to have some fun.

Across the wide desert the Dinosaurs stomped,
Over the sand they roared and they romped.

Then Georgie and Dee – and Cat too –
All danced together in the Hullabaloo!

Jaws CLASHED! Claws FLASHED!
Faster and faster, feet CRASHED!

Over the volcano the Dinosaurs jumped,
Down its side they thundered and thumped.

Jaws CLASHED! Claws FLASHED!
Louder and louder, feet SMASHED!

The land shook with fearsome roars,
"This is the DANCE OF THE DINOSAURS!"

Suddenly, down they all tumbled into a pile.
"The storm is over," whispered Cat with a smile.

"I'm tired," yawned Georgie, "is it time for bed?"
And everyone nodded a sleepy head.

Then all the Dinosaurs waved good-bye!
And off they sailed across the starry sky.

Through the hush of the peaceful night
Homewards they flew in the twinkling light.

"Look," said Cat, "we've not far to go."
And they saw their house far below.

Back they drifted over whispering trees,
Then landed softly in the gentle breeze.

"Hush, be quiet," said Cat, as in they hurried.
Then quickly back up the stairs they scurried.

Into their soft beds they quietly crept,
And soon Georgie and Dee and Cat - they slept.

And far, far away...

...The Dinosaurs dreamt under the starlight
Of another Dance on another night...